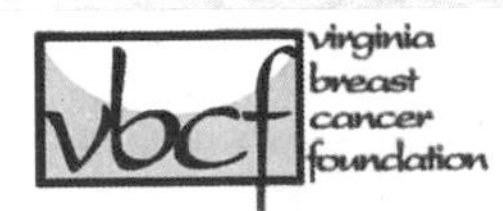
vbcf
virginia
breast
cancer
foundation

For my sons Sergio and Javier, and dedicated to all the mothers in the world—first and foremost, my own.

My sincerest thanks to Dr. Javier Hornedo for his tenacity and wisdom, and for having allowed me to use his name for the General in this story.

All of the author's royalties from this book will go to the international program *"ponte guapa te sentirás mejor"* in support of women with cancer, promoted by the Stanpa Foundation.

Mom Goes to War

Calle Claveles 10 | Urb Monteclaro | Pozuelo de Alarcón
28223 Madrid | Spain | www.cuentodeluz.com
Original title in Spanish: Mamá se va a la guerra
English translation by Jon Brokenbrow
Light Series
ISBN: 978-84-15503-20-0
Printed by Shanghai Chenxi Printing Co., Ltd. in PRC, April 2012, print number 1273-08

Irene Aparici Martín

Mom Goes to War

Illustrated by Mónica Carretero

Once upon a time there were two young princes called James and Simon. Long ago, their parents, the King and queen, had decided to separate their Kingdoms. The boys went to a special school for little princes, because one day they too would rule their own Kingdoms. One morning, the queen called them to her throne room. This was where she normally met with her ministers.

"James," said Prince Simon, the eldest brother, "something serious must be going on if Mom wants to see us in the throne room. What have you been up to?"

When they arrived, the King was there too.

"Uh-oh, Dad's there too—now we're in trouble!" said Prince Simon, pushing his brother forward. But the queen, with a serious expression on her face, walked towards them and hugged them lovingly. She looked at each prince in turn and then at the King. She invited them to sit down, and began to speak in a calm, serious voice.

"Boys, I have to talk to you about something very important. We have a rebellion on our hands."

"A rebellion?" asked the princes, with worried expressions.

"Yes," said the queen, glancing over at the King.

"Listen to me very carefully," she said. "My lookouts have detected some groups of dangerous rebels who are moving around in gangs. They want to invade my Kingdom. I've called the King because he's always an ally, and even though this is a battle I've got to win on my own, between the two of us we'll make sure that you're always safe."

"But what kind of battle is that? Where are these rebels from? Are you sure you're going to win?" The princes couldn't ask their questions fast enough.

"Well, my battle is called breast cancer, and the rebels are cells that are multiplying out of control. But you shouldn't be afraid, because there are medicines that can wipe them out forever."

"So you're going to get better?" asked Prince James.

"Yes, I'm going to get better, but it's not going to be easy. You see, this is going to be a big battle, so I've called for the very finest soldiers in the world to help me out. One of them is a general who's fought in a lot of wars like mine. He's very wise, and he's worked out a strategy for me to win. If I go along with it, he says I'm almost sure to succeed."

Prince Simon wriggled uncomfortably in his seat, while Prince James, who was a little younger, relaxed when he heard that their mother would get better.

After a brief pause, the queen continued in her gentle, quiet voice.

"Now we're preparing the army for the battle. General Hornedo will be in command. I trust him completely. We are working on our strategy together. Do you want to know what we're going to do?"

"Yes!" shouted the princes. "Can we fight too?"

"Of course!" laughed the queen. But then her face became serious again. "But not on the front lines, because you are still young. You will be at the rear, making sure that I'm calm and relaxed, so that I can concentrate on the battle and on keeping the barracks clean and tidy. I'll keep you informed about how the war is going."

Then the king spoke: "You'll still come to visit me at my castle, and when the queen needs extra peace and quiet, then you can come and see me too."

The little princes gradually relaxed. The queen continued to talk.

"You see, my body is going to be the battlefield. Some of my cells, like my red and white blood cells, are my army," she said.

"But in the body, there are other cells who lead peaceful lives, good cells who are just trying to get on with their jobs, but who unfortunately are going to get caught up in this battle. They are the cells that make my stomach and my lungs work, and they make sure that my bones are strong and that I have a clear mind."

"In some parts of the body, like the groin, the neck or the armpits, we have watchtowers. They are called ganglions. In these watchtowers I have the best lookouts. A few days ago, we received a coded message from Tower Number One in my left armpit. You saw that my arm had swollen up: that was the alarm signal. From the decoding room, they passed the message on to General Hornedo."

The queen pulled out a letter, and began to read:

"Towers One and Two are being attacked by armed rebels. They are a very strange bunch. They look like normal citizens because they are dressed like everyone else, but they're crazy! They all shout "hup!" and start to multiply. We're putting up a fight, but we need reinforcements."

When the queen had finished reading, she looked up at the princes, who were listening attentively. She continued to explain her strategy.

"The General has sent spy planes all around my body, but especially my left breast, because that's where we think most of these rebels are hiding out. My breast is like a thick jungle, full of trees, lakes and caves. It's a perfect place for the rebels to hide. But our planes are equipped with the very latest technology; they've got ultra-sensitive cameras with gamma rays that can take photos in even the darkest places."

"The other day, we sent a group of parachutists on a special mission to the jungle. They managed to capture some of the rebels. Now we're holding them in a special laboratory, interrogating them to find out everything they know. We've already discovered that they're very dangerous types indeed. They don't worry about burning the fields and forcing others to join them. So we've got to capture them all, and I know this sounds terrible, but we have to get rid of them all, because once they go over to the rebel side, there's no way of curing them, and they can do a lot of harm," she told the boys.

The princes listened carefully to the queen's story.

"We think that some of the rebels have slipped past the lookout tower and have escaped onto the motorways and roads, which are my lymph and blood vessels that lead to other parts of the kingdom. They camouflage themselves so well, and there are still so few of them, that the traffic police—my red and white blood cells—still haven't detected them."

"So how are you going to capture them and get rid of them?" asked the little princes.

"Well, the General has gotten in touch with an American factory that makes special defense weapons. They've developed some new devices that are really effective," answered the queen.

"The trouble is that they're quite difficult to handle," she told her sons. There's a medicine called Scalpozap, and others that are called Extermamide and Demolozine."

"Demolo...what?" stammered Prince James.

"I know, they've got very strange names!" the queen agreed. "That's to prevent industrial espionage. We're going to start with Scalpozap. Once a week, a delivery will arrive in my body. The soldier cells will pick up these weapons and travel through my blood to hunt down the rebels. Most of them will go to lookout towers one and two, but others will keep patrolling the rest of my body. Scalpozap has a type of flashlight that turns on when it detects the rebel cells, and changes the color of their clothes, and then, **KERPOW!** It leaves the rebels completely out of action so they can't keep multiplying or contaminate the other cells with their nonsense. I know that some of my own cells will die in the process, and that's why I might feel more tired than usual.
And there's another problem..."

"What?" asked the little princes, worriedly.

"Well, the cells that make my hair grow will die as well. They're innocent, hard-working cells, and it's a shame they have to go, but the medicine will change the color of their clothes too, and so far nobody's invented a better weapon."

"But you'll be really ugly!", Prince Simon cried. The queen stood up, regally adjusted her crown and said in a very serious voice, "My little princes, I am going to the battlefront. I'm not going there to look pretty: I'm going there to fight. Fortunately, you don't need your hair to stay alive. But there are a lot of beautiful bald people in the world, and anyway, once the war is over, the cells that make my hair grow will come back."

"And how long will it last?" Prince Simon wanted to know.

"The first stage, with the Scalpozap, will last for three months. When that stage ends, the General will send me the rangers and the spy planes to find out how things are going. I imagine that things will be calmer in the towers, and most of the rebels will have been knocked off their feet."

"And that's it?"

"No, we'll have to be very patient. After the Scalpozap, we'll move on to the next stage, with much more powerful defensive weapons. Listen carefully, because this is very important: every three weeks, a plane will arrive on a secret mission, loaded with missiles with Extermamide and Demolozine. They are lethal to the rebels and will destroy them, but they will also kill a lot of allies, because they are bombs that can't distinguish between the good guys and the bad guys," said the queen.

"But why do innocent cells have to die?" said Prince Simon.

"It's hard for me too, my dear. I don't want innocent lives to be lost, but you must remember that the rebels hide amongst them, and attack everyone who gets in their way. We've searched for the best weapons in the world, not only because they get rid of the rebels, but because they're the most selective. But we can't avoid some kind of collateral damage."

The queen hugged the young prince. He still had so much to learn!

Prince James was getting impatient. "Please mother, tell us more."

"This stage will also last three months. I imagine that by then I'll be really tired, but you shouldn't be too worried, because if a lot of my soldiers die, we can ask our allies for reinforcements. Fortunately, I'm good friends with a lot of countries who are ready to help."

"What a long battle! When will it end?" asked the princes.

"Yes, boys, it will be a long battle, but if we get through stage one and stage two successfully, then it will be over."

"How many stages are left?"

"Next, a special group of soldiers will move into action. These soldiers are responsible for cleaning up the battlefield, especially the towers and my breast. They are called surgeons, and they'll get rid of all of the rebels, dead or alive, who are still there. It will be a quick mission that only lasts a few hours, although I'll need to be in the hospital for a few days to recover from it."

"And that's it?" Prince James asked again.

"Very nearly. Then the war will almost be over. We will just have to put the final stage into action, which involves burning down all of the places where the rebels have been hiding out. For that, we'll use very powerful defensive weapons."

"Giant bombs? Why do you need to do that?" exclaimed Prince Simon, who apart from being very clever, had inherited a special sensitivity from his mother.

"No, they're not giant bombs, but close!" reassured the queen, trying to calm down her son. "We use very powerful methods to prevent cells being born that might turn into rebels one day. This stage is also quite long, a couple of months, and the worst thing is that I'll probably end up without the lookout towers. After the battle they will be very damaged, and we'll have to pull them down. But then," said the queen, raising her hands, "the battle will finally be over!"

The little princes sat quietly, thinking to themselves. Prince James, who had always been the most inquisitive and imaginative of the two, asked, "And then what will happen?"

The queen smiled. She liked the fact that her children were curious and always asked questions. They would be excellent kings when they grew up.

"Well, the same thing that happens in every kingdom when there's been a battle. At first, all of the people and the soldiers are tired, the fields have been burned and there aren't any crops, people are hungry, and the survivors cry over the loved ones they've lost. But little by little, everything goes back to normal. New children are born who will never know that there was a battle, and like all children, they will fill their homes with happiness. Their parents will go back to work, and the kingdom will go back to being just the way it was. We will have learned our lesson, and we'll be more watchful to make sure the rebels never try to invade again."

There was a long silence. It was a lot of information for the boys to take in.

And then the king spoke: "I think the queen has explained everything very well, but you mustn't worry, and if there's anything you don't understand, or anything that concerns you, you must tell us, because we're all in this battle together so that we can win."

The princes quietly nodded their heads. And then the queen stood up, and said: "So now, my little princes, if you don't have any more questions, I want you to swear your oath of loyalty to the queen. You need to know that even though I have to fight on the battlefront, I will still be in control of the kingdom, and everything will be as normal as possible. We have a lot of friends and allies who will be by our side, cheering on our troops, and making sure I'm in good spirits. And although at times I'll have to be with the soldiers because I'm the queen, remember that above everything else I am your mother, and I love you dearly."